Ick and Crud

Going t...

by Wiley Blevins • illustrated by Jim Paillot

RED CHAIR
PRESS

Funny Bone Books

and Funny Bone Readers are produced and published by

Red Chair Press LLC   PO Box 333   South Egremont, MA 01258-0333

www.redchairpress.com

About the Author

Wiley Blevins has taught elementary school in both the United States and South America. He has also written over 60 books for children and 15 for teachers, as well as created reading programs for schools in the U.S. and Asia with Scholastic, Macmillan/McGraw-Hill, Houghton-Mifflin Harcourt, and other publishers. Wiley currently lives and writes in New York City.

About the Artist

Jim Paillot is a dad, husband and illustrator. He lives in Arizona with his family and two dogs and any other animal that wants to come in out of the hot sun. When not illustrating, Jim likes to hike, watch cartoons and collect robots.

Publisher's Cataloging-In-Publication Data
(Prepared by The Donohue Group, Inc.)

Names: Blevins, Wiley. | Paillot, Jim, illustrator.
Title: Ick and Crud. Book 3, Going to the vet / by Wiley Blevins ; illustrated by Jim Paillot.
Other Titles: Going to the vet

Description: South Egremont, MA : Red Chair Press, [2017] | Series: First chapters | Interest age level: 005-007. | Summary: "Bob is loading the car for a trip. Yippee! Ick and Crud love to take trips. But suddenly this trip doesn't seem like it will be fun."--Provided by publisher.

Identifiers: LCCN 2016947353 | ISBN 978-1-63440-187-6 (library hardcover) | ISBN 978-1-63440-190-6 (paperback) | ISBN 978-1-63440-193-7 (ebook)

Subjects: LCSH: Friendship--Juvenile fiction. | Veterinarians--Juvenile fiction. | Dogs--Juvenile fiction. | CYAC: Friendship--Fiction. | Veterinarians--Fiction. | Dogs--Fiction.

Classification: LCC PZ7.B618652 Icg 2017 (print) | LCC PZ7.B618652 (ebook) | DDC [E]--dc23

Printed in the United States of America
0517 1P CGBF17

Table of Contents

Meet the Characters

Crud

Ick

Miss Puffy

Bob

Be Strong!

Bob set out two small crates.
Ick and Crud knew what that meant.
A trip to Grandma Bob's house.
Or, the vet!

"I'm not falling for that again," said Ick.
Ick and Crud backed away. Bob tossed a
bone into each crate. "Be strong," said Crud.

"But it looks so tasty," said Ick.
"I can almost feel the crunch."

"It's just a trick," said Crud.

Ick inched closer to the crate.
He sniffed. The dog bone smell
filled his nose.

"Don't do it!" begged Crud.

But in walked Ick. *Snap!* The crate
door slammed shut and locked.

Crud buried his head under his paws.
"Was it worth it?" he asked.

Ick gnawed on his bone and shook his
head up and down.

"Okay, buddy," said Crud. "For you,
I'll go where no dog should ever go."
Crud took slow puppy-steps into the
other crate. His head hung low.

Snap! The door slammed shut.

Not a Fun Ride

Bob grabbed the crates and loaded them into his car. Ick liked car rides much more than Crud did. Ick liked to bark at the other cars, at kids walking by, and at the shadow of his tail.

Ick also liked to hang his head out the window. He liked the way his tongue flapped in the air. But not this time. Not in this crate. So he just barked and barked and barked.

"Can you please stop yapping?" asked Crud. "I have a headache now."

"The vet can take care of that," said Ick. And he kept on barking. Down Maple Street. Up Elm Street. Across Main Street. And all around the town. Until they got to the place they feared most. The vet.

Ick tried to bark to show Bob what a bad thing he had done. But instead of a *woof*, he could barely squeak out a *woo*. Crud liked that.

"Let's get you two inside," said Bob. "The vet is waiting."

He pushed open the office door. A lady with hair like a French Poodle's greeted them. "Have a seat," she said and pointed.

Bob unlatched the crates. Out tumbled
Ick and Crud. They looked at the only
empty seat. Beside it sat Mrs. Martin. On
her lap Miss Puffy posed, licking her paws
like they were lollipops.

"Oh, *ick*," said Ick.

"Oh, *crud*," said Crud. "Do you think
she saw us?"

"Hello, boys," purred Miss Puffy.

"She saw us," whispered Ick.

"Are you here for your shots?" asked Miss Puffy.

"Shots?" cried Ick. "Oh, no. No, no, no, no, no-no-no-no-no."

"Don't listen to her," said Crud. "I'm sure it's just a check-up."

"Of course," said Miss Puffy and she hissed a laugh.

"I'm here to get my picture taken,"
she said. "The vet is making his calendar
for next year. I'll be January."

Crud rolled his eyes. "What a sad start
to the year," he whispered. Then he looked
away.

In the window Crud spotted a turtle. He barked *hello*.

He would have called out the turtle's name. But he didn't know if the turtle had one. The turtle never said. So, Crud called him *Turtle*. It was better than calling him *Pickles*, which is what Ick wanted to call him.

"Look who's here," Crud said.

Ick lifted his paw in a wave. "Now I want to eat a pickle," he moaned.

Turtle slowly lifted his head and winked. Crud was sure he heard the little turtle giggle. As he turned around, he found out why.

The vet stood in the doorway. In his hand was the largest needle Crud had ever seen.

No Way, Bob!

"Yowza!" said Crud.

"Uh-oh," said Ick.

"Ick and Crud," the vet called. "You're next."

Ick darted under Bob's chair. "Come on boys," said the vet. Ick grabbed onto the chair leg.

22

"Come on," said Crud. "I'm not going in there alone."

"Nope. Not gonna do it," Ick said. "You go ahead and tell me about it later. Send me an email."

"Bad times are never so bad with a friend by your side" said Crud. "Or at least that's what Bob always says."

"This chair leg is my only friend now," said Ick.

He licked the leg. Bob squatted. "Come on, boy" he said. He grabbed for Ick. "No way, Bob!" cried Ick.

With Bob on the floor, Crud saw his chance to escape. He took off for the front door.

Bob jumped to his feet and scooped
him up just in time. Then Bob tugged on
Ick's collar. "Come on, boy," he said.

Ick kicked his paws all the way to the
big white room.

"Have fun," purred Miss Puffy.

Bad, Bad, Bad!

Once inside, the vet quickly shut the door. "Who's first?" he asked and waved the needle in his hand.

"It's just so big," said Ick, staring at the needle.

"You can go first," said Crud. "I don't mind."

"It's just so big," said Ick again.

"Go on, Ick," said Crud. "I insist."

Crud slipped behind him. The vet
reached down to grab Ick. But Ick rolled
on his side, did a backflip, and landed
behind Crud.

Then he pushed Crud toward the vet.
"Sorry, buddy," he whispered.

The vet scooped Crud up, plopped him on the table, and plunged the needle into his hairy butt.

"OWWW… WEEEE!" yelled Crud. "Bad vet! Bad, bad, bad!"

Ick froze. The vet handed Crud a bone and put him down. Then he reached for Ick and lifted him onto the table.

"It's just so big," Ick mumbled.
He grabbed his butt. "Oh, the horror,"
Ick moaned. "Why oh why did I look?"

Crud gnawed on his bone and didn't
look up. "Help me, Crud. I'm too young to
die. I'm too pretty to die. I'm too cuddly
to die. I have so many more squirrels to
chase. And so many more flowers to pee
on. Oh, the horror!"

The vet plopped Ick back onto the floor and handed him a small bone. "What just happened?" asked Ick.

"You got a shot," said Crud.

"When?" asked Ick.

"When you were crying like a scaredy pup," said Crud.

"I don't cry," said Ick. Then he looked back at his butt. "It was just so big," he said. "I shouldn't have looked."

"But you didn't feel a thing," said Crud. "So, will you go first next time?" Ick shook his head.

"Is that a *yes*?" asked Crud.

"That would be a *no*," said Ick.

"Are you sure?" asked Crud.

"As sure as I know that the only good day is a day with you," said Ick.

"Okay, buddy. Then let's go home," said Crud.

They both hopped into their crates and happily chewed their yummy bones all the way home. Even though neither could sit down.